COP. 1

398.2 Aruego, Jose
ARU
      A crocodile's tale

~~Ramsay~~

F

DATE			
BV			
allmitt			
Frady 7			
BV 82			
F.R.C			
Aarrington			

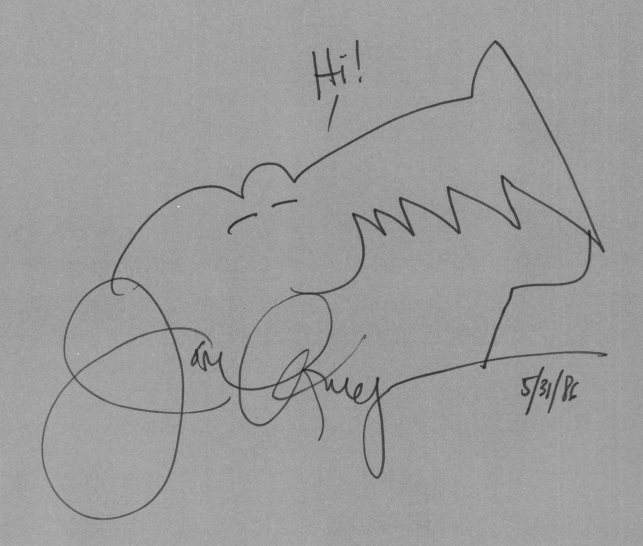

A CROCODILE'S TALE

To My Father

A CROCODILE'S TALE

A Philippine Folk Story by
JOSE & ARIANE ARUEGO

Charles Scribner's Sons, New York

398.2
ARU
COP. 1

Copyright © 1972 Jose Aruego

This book published simultaneously in the United States of America and in Canada - Copyright under the Berne Convention

All rights reserved. No part of this book may be reproduced in any form without the permission of Charles Scribner's Sons.

3 5 7 9 11 13 15 17 19   RD/C   20 18 16 14 12 10 8 6 4 2

Printed in the United States of America
Library of Congress Catalog Card Number 75-37185
SBN 684-12806-3 (Trade cloth, RB)

One day when Juan was walking near the river, he heard someone crying.

Looking around, he saw a crocodile tied to a tree.
"Can I help you?" Juan asked.

"If you free me, I will give you a gold ring,"
said the crocodile.

Juan untied the rope and asked,
"May I please have the ring now?"

"I don't have it with me," replied the crocodile.
"Jump on my back and we will get it."

As soon as they reached the middle of the river,
the crocodile said, "I don't have a gold ring.
And now I am going to eat you up!"

"That isn't fair!" cried Juan.
"You can't eat me. I just saved your life."

The crocodile laughed. "Most boys never have the chance to be eaten by a crocodile."

Just then an old basket came floating by.
"Please, let's ask that basket if you
should eat me or not," Juan begged.

"If you like," agreed the crocodile.

"Basket, basket," Juan called. "Please settle an argument for us. I found this crocodile in a trap. He promised me a gold ring if I would free him. But when I untied the rope, he said he didn't have a gold ring, and that he would eat me.
Do you call that gratitude?"

"When I was new," said the basket, "I carried rice to market for my master, and fruit for his wife, and I played games with their son. But when I became old, they threw me away."

"People are not grateful, crocodile, so why should you be? Go ahead and eat him," said the basket.

"Thank you," replied the crocodile. "I will."

"No!" cried Juan. He looked around, and seeing a hat floating nearby, called to it.

"What's the matter?" asked the hat.

"I heard this crocodile crying because he was caught,"
Juan answered. "I freed him and now he wants to eat me.
Do you think that is right?"

"When I was new," said the hat, "my master wore me
proudly to the city. I shaded him from the sun
while he worked and kept him dry when it rained.
But when I became old, he threw me into the river."

"People are not grateful, so why should you be?
Go ahead and eat him, crocodile," said the hat.

"Did you hear that?" said the crocodile,
opening his mouth to swallow the boy.

"No, not yet!" cried Juan.
"Let's ask that monkey
in the banana tree over there."

"All right, but hurry,"
said the crocodile impatiently.
"This is your last chance."

"Monkey, monkey!" Juan shouted.
"This crocodile is going to eat me!"
"I can't hear you!" the monkey shouted back.
"Come a little closer."

The crocodile swam toward the bank.
Juan yelled, "This crocodile was caught—"

"I still can't hear you," called the monkey.
"Can't you come a little closer?"

The crocodile grumbled, "I just want to eat this boy,"
as he swam closer to the bank.

Just then, Juan jumped onto the bank and was safe.
"Oh, thank you," he said to the monkey.
"You have saved my life and I'll always be grateful."

"Then maybe you'll do me a favor," said the monkey.
"If you could persuade your father to plant more
bananas, there would be plenty for all of us.
And when you see me in his trees,
will you close your eyes and not tell on me?"

"All right," said Juan.

The End

UPPER LYNN ELEMENTARY SCHOOL
1540 COLEMAN ST.
NORTH VANCOUVER, B. C.